The Spiders

By Jack Gabolinscy

Illustrated by Marten Coombe

Michael sat watching TV. Above him, a tiny brown spider began letting itself down from the ceiling, like a lone mountaineer hang-gliding down a cliff face. Its little legs waved around, looking for something solid to rest on. Curling itself into a ball it hung . . . a tiny black pendulum swinging gently in the breeze.

Stretching for another brownie from the kitchen table, Michael laid down on the couch. The commercial finished, and he concentrated again on the movie. Meanwhile, the spider wound itself down some more—slowly this time—in one long continuous movement.

For the next ten minutes, Michael lay watching TV; the spider continued to climb down its thread.

Spiders

When the movie ended, Michael stretched and yawned. His glance fell on the spider, now just above his head. He watched its hairy legs scrub against each other.

A frown turned down the corners of Michael's mouth. He hated spiders. The spider, knowing it was near the end of its descent, began spinning out its thread faster. It was almost on Michael's nose before he brushed a finger across the thread. He sat up with the spider hanging from his finger. The spider didn't seem to realize what had happened. It continued to climb downward. When it was almost on the coffee table, Michael switched the thread to his other hand. Again, the spider patiently spun its thread and climbed downward. Michael laughed. "Stupid thing!" he said. He held the spider over his glass of water and dropped it in.

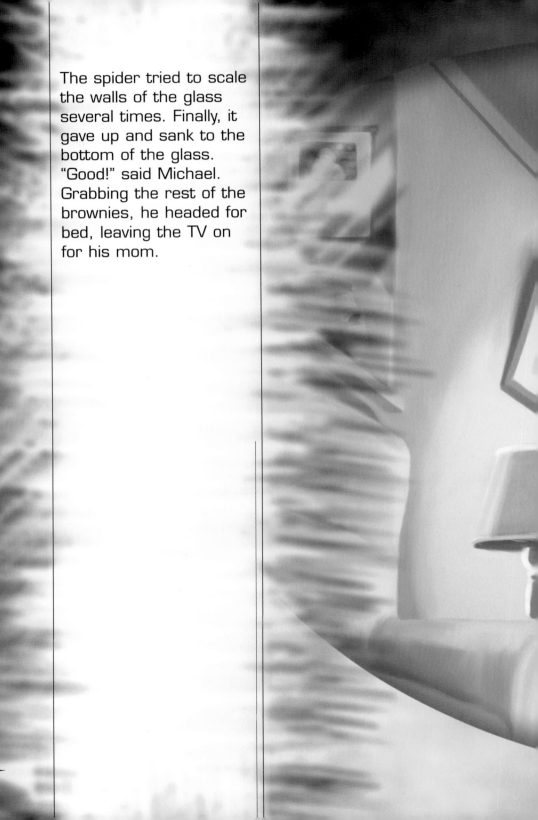

The spider tried to scale the walls of the glass several times. Finally, it gave up and sank to the bottom of the glass. "Good!" said Michael. Grabbing the rest of the brownies, he headed for bed, leaving the TV on for his mom.

Scale the walls
What does
this mean?

Question

Ten minutes later, there was a faint scraping from beneath the living room door. Two long black legs, followed by a big head and an even bigger hairier body and six more legs appeared. It scurried to the darkness beneath a chair where it squatted, its eight eyes looking around the room for danger. Satisfied all was quiet, it moved toward the tiny round corpse inside the glass.

Seconds later, two more spiders scuttled under the door. Another appeared like magic from the back of the TV, and two more big black hairy ones rushed in from behind the bookcases.

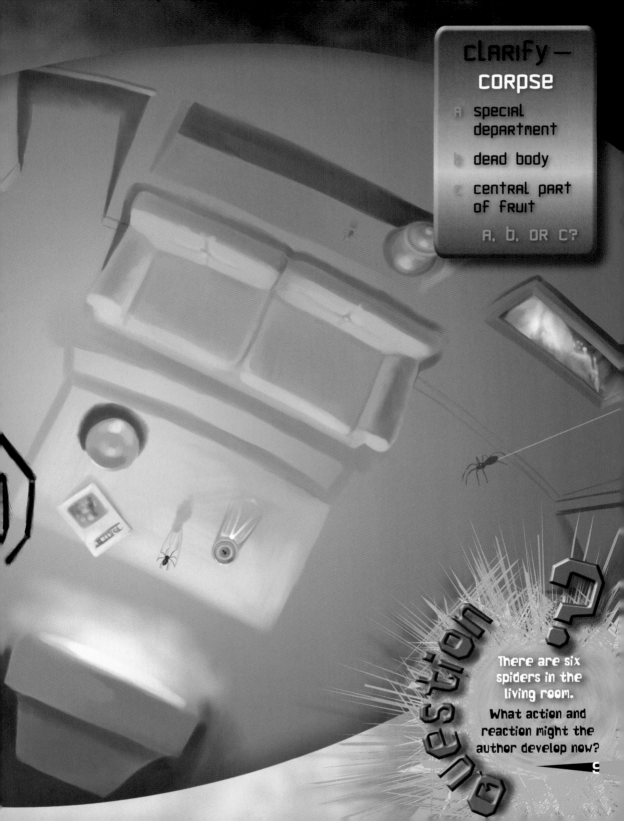

CLARIFY —
CORPSE

a special
   department

b dead body

c central part
   of fruit

A, b, OR C?

Question?

There are six
spiders in the
living room.
What action and
reaction might the
author develop now?

Silently, the six spiders formed a circle around the dead spider in the glass. Then, as one, they raised their front legs and began a sad dance around the corpse.

Back and forth, around and around the spiders went. First one way and then back the other.

Every minute or two, they stopped, motionless and silent, like mourners at a funeral.

A long time passed while the sad dance continued. Then the biggest spider started toward the door with its five friends marching in a single line behind it.

CLARIFY –
MOURNERS

a GRIEVING
ATTENDANTS
AT A FUNERAL

b VISITORS

c PASSERS-BY

A, b, OR C?

Like silent mourners at a funeral

Simile or Metaphor?

A simile compares one thing to another by using the words "like" or "as," and often creates a mental picture in the reader's mind.

A metaphor compares one thing to another without using the words "like" or "as," and often creates a mental picture in the reader's mind.

11

The next morning, as usual, Michael woke early. Uncurling his body, he rolled on his back, stretching and rubbing his eyes. For a few moments he lay still, thinking. He groaned. It was Monday. Time to get dressed for school. He opened his drawers to get clean socks. Inside, he discovered a huge web—thick, gray, and sticky—surrounding his socks. "Yuck!" he said.

It was then that he discovered that his shoes were filled with webs, too. Thick bushy webs that determinedly stuck to his fingers. Webs that clung to his clothes when he tried to wipe them off and that smudged into a sticky mess when he tried to remove them with the clothes brush.

He groaned.
It was Monday.

What inference can
be made from this?

Inference:

Personification:

[Personification: likening of human
characteristics to things and ideas]

Thick bushy webs that determinedly
stuck to his fingers.

Is this personification?

13

After breakfast, Michael's mom ran the vacuum over his clothes. He rushed out to the garage to get his bike and got his first really big scare of the day. His bike was a mass of sticky gray webs. The handlebars were covered. The chain and pedals were covered. The frame and wheels were tangled in densely clustered sticky threads. The whole bike seemed to be tied to the shed wall by thousands of sticky gray lines.

It was as if the bike had been unused for hundreds of years, not just a couple of days.

A thoughtful frown wrinkled his forehead as Michael swept the bike clean with the shed broom and hosed it down with water.

Descriptive Language

Language that paints a **visual** picture:

Mass of sticky gray   Densely clustered

Find some more descriptive language!

Late for school, Michael had to hurry to his room and put his books in his desk. That was his second big scare of the day. He opened his desk lid and let out a shrill cry—"Ooooo!"

Spiders scattered from his desk. They ran across the lid, down the legs, and across the floor. Big, black, hairy spiders. One—bigger, blacker, hairier, and uglier than the rest—walked slowly as if it didn't have a care in the world. It stared right at him, daring him to do something. In his desk, webs stuck to the books and tangled around the pens. They hung from the lid and dangled down the legs.

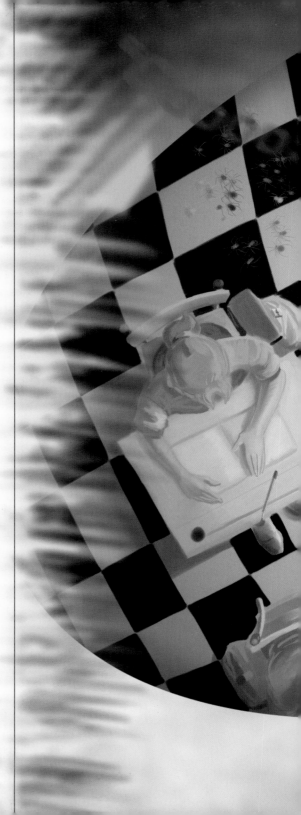

Which words best describe the emotions Michael might be feeling?

excitement
panic   ALARM
CALMNESS   fear
dread   apprehension
serenity

At lunchtime, Michael was still upset. He ate his lunch by himself. He opened his lunch box carefully, and received his third big shock of the day . . . his lunch was encased in webs. The webs were so thick, he could barely see his sandwich. He knew then—without a doubt—that the spiders were playing tricks on him.

For the rest of the day, Michael was almost too frightened to do anything . . .

. . .too frightened to open his desk.

. . .too frightened to get the paints from the cupboard when asked by the teacher.

He was almost too scared to get his bike at the end of the day.

CLARIFY —
encased

a lightly covered

b topped by

c completely
enclosed by

A, b, OR c?

question ?

Why do you think Michael ate lunch by himself?

19

Michael rode home from school thoughtfully. His mom was in the yard, so he went into the kitchen for a drink. Suddenly he realized the kitchen was very dark. Looking up, he discovered the windows were covered with spider webs that hung down like curtains. In the middle of each web squatted a huge black spider.

Everywhere he looked there were spiders. They hung from walls and squatted on the chair, their front legs seemingly pointing at him in accusation. His throat went tight. His spine tingled. He reached for the door handle, but whipped his hand away fast when he saw a spider sitting there with its legs pointing at him.

ACTION	REACTION
he looked up and discovered the windows covered with spider webs	?
he reached for the door handle	?

Spiders' webs hanging like curtains.

A simile compares one thing to another by using the words "like" or "as," and often creates a mental picture in the reader's mind.

A metaphor compares one thing to another without using the words "like" or "as," and often creates a mental picture in the reader's mind.

Simile or Metaphor?

Inference:

Their front legs were pointing at him in accusation.

What inference can be made from this?

21

Michael ran into the living room and fell back onto the sofa. Then, as one, the spiders began to dance . . . a strange monotonous dance.

Back and forth,
back and forth,
around and around.

Their horrible rasping, scraping sound grew louder and more ghastly as they danced faster and faster. Their front legs began stomping. Angry little pistons rising and stomping. Hundreds of them in unison.

Bang, bang, bang!

Quicker and louder and even more demanding . . .

CLARIFY —
monotonous

a slow and sad

b tedious and
    repetitive

c continuous

A, b, or C?

Imagery – The use of words by the writer to create a mind picture

Angry little pistons rising and stomping

[Use the imagery of the text to create a mind picture]

23

Bang, bang, bang!
Bang, **bang, bang**!

"Wake up, Michael!"

Michael opened his frightened eyes, expecting to see the spiders advancing on him. Instead, he saw Mom through the glass in the front door. "Let me in!"

Bang, bang, bang!

The door from the yard had blown shut and locked.

Compare & contrast — Michael's Emotions

Spiders dancing	Mom at door
terrified	?
guilty	?
panic	?

Michael looked around. Everything was back to normal. He felt safe when Mom asked him the same old questions about his day at dinner that night. She pointed to his sleeve. "What's that?" she asked.

Michael looked down. A small black spider was jiggling its way down his arm. "It's just a little spinning spider, Mom. A little spinning spider."

"Get rid of it!" shrieked Mom. "You know I don't like spiders."

Michael grinned. "It's all right, Mom. A little spider never hurt anyone."

Select the main points you would include in a summary of the *The Spiders*.

- michael is at home watching television.

- michael ate brownies.

- michael dropped a spider into a glass of water.

- six spiders appeared and performed a strange dance around the dead spider.

- the spider's eight eyes looked around the room for danger.

- michael ate lunch by himself.

- michael discovered spiders' webs everywhere.

- the spider's front legs began stomping.

- michael's mother woke him from his dream.

- mom asked him questions about his day.

- michael changed his attitude toward spiders.

27

Making connections – Talk about emotions, situations, or characters that you met in *The Spiders*.

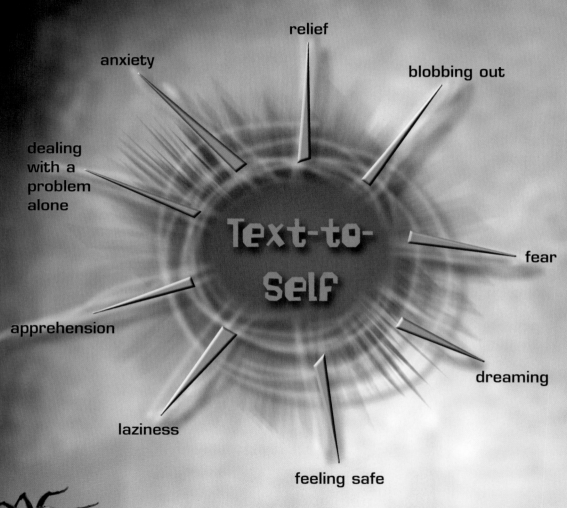

relief

anxiety

blobbing out

dealing with a problem alone

Text-to-Self

fear

apprehension

dreaming

laziness

feeling safe

Talk about other stories
you may have read that
have similar features.
Compare the stories.

Text-to-World

Talk about situations in
the world that might
connect to elements in
the story.

Planning a short story ...

Decide on a storyline

A boy killed a spider in a glass of water.

Spiders came and held a ceremonial dance around the dead spider. They made webs in the boy's things.

The boy realized he shouldn't kill spiders thoughtlessly.

Think about the character or characters

Think about the way a character will **think**, *act*, and **feel**. Make some short notes or quick sketches.

became scared of spiders

thoughtless in actions

Make some short notes.

location

time

atmosphere

Decide on the events in order

Michael sat watching TV. Above him, a tiny brown spider began letting itself down from the ceiling, like a lone mountaineer hang-gliding down a cliff face.

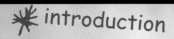 introduction

events

Everywhere he looked there were spiders. They hung from walls and squatted on the chair, their front legs seemingly pointing at him in accusation. His throat went tight. His spine tingled.

climax

31

Short stories usually have:

- A short introduction that grabs the reader's interest

- A single fast-moving plot with no sidetracks

- Fewer characters that are briefly described, but who still appear real to the reader

- Well-chosen words that quickly draw the setting and atmosphere

- A climax that occurs late